I0537587

HOLIDAY IN PARADISE

S Cuppari

S CUPPARI
www.scuppari.com

First published in Australia by
S Cuppari - www.scuppari.com -
in 2013 as part of the
S Cuppari Romance Minis.

© S Cuppari 2013

Large Print:
ISBN-10: 097508898X
ISBN-13: 978-0-9750889-8-2

Printed by Lulu.com.

No part of this book may be reproduced
in part or whole in any other medium
without written permission.

CONTENTS

Welcome to your very own
S Cuppari Romance Mini!

S Cuppari Romance Minis is a new romance line
dedicated to reading romances on the go
as they are romance novellas jampacked
with romance, mystery and adventure and
are based in exotic locations around the world.

ABOUT THE AUTHOR

S Cuppari has been in publishing for over ten years and
has published many magazine titles such as *Writing Edge*
and *Take a Break Reads* as well as book series like *Metro
Seven Pacific Heat* by Jade Mansfield. S Cuppari has
also written for different publications as well as edited
and authored books.

   If you would like to connect with S Cuppari you can
surf to the official site at scuppari.com, the official blog
at scuppari.tumblr.com, like the Facebook page at
www.facebook.com/SCuppari or follow at Twitter
@s_cuppari.

1

The Fiesta

The music filled the room, people were chatting loudly, and her friends were all dancing, but Sabina Callaway had eyes fixed only on her husband, Max. It was their twenty-fifth wedding anniversary and Max Callaway had thrown Sabina a surprise party at the Club de Fiesta to celebrate their years of marriage. She often considered herself the luckiest woman in the world and although their life together had begun difficultly, she wouldn't change it for the world. No, in Sabina's mind, Max was the greatest husband.

Max walked up to the front of the club and whispered something in the DJ's ear, he smiled as the DJ changed songs. Sabina held her breath as the song No Woman like You came onto the speakers. That was their song, it was playing the day that Max Callaway and Sabina Calli found the treasure - monetarily and metaphorically. Yes, it was that day that the two of them saved the treasure from bad guys and found the most important treasure of all - love.

Sabina found herself lost in thought about that day, when her husband came and did a curtsy in front of her. "May I have this dance, milady?" he asked in a phony British accent.

She grinned. "Certainly, dear. My, this

dance, it brings back such memories…"

He wrapped his arms around her neck. "The greatest of memories is nothing compared to the present I have standing before me, you, my dear, are spectacular."

She bit her lip in the same way that she always did when he complimented her, she became as a teenager again when he spoke to her. Sabina reached up and kissed his nose. "I love you."

"And, I have loved you since that day."

At that moment, their fifteen year old daughter, Rosa, came behind them and began to laugh. "Oh Mum, Dad, you guys are still like teenagers, can you share with the crowd all about how you met and fell in love?" Rosa handed the microphone to her father.

"Well... umm..." He gazed at his beautiful wife and smiled. "It is quite a story. Sabina was only twenty-two years old..."

Sabina Calli and her two best friends Marla and Lydia practically jumped off the plane when it had landed on the tarmac at Bauerfield International Airport in Port Villa, Vanuatu. The year was 1988 and the young women had just graduated from college with BAs in Journalism. Marla had secured a job working as an entry level advice columnist for a teen magazine, Lydia had gotten a job working as a weather reporter for a local news network, but

Sabina had yet to find a job.

The women had come to Vanuatu for a vacation before their jobs started, however, Sabina was there for the entire summer—she was worn out from the job search and needed a change of scenery.

Disappointed as she was, Sabina wanted to support Marla and Lydia as they celebrated their new jobs. After all, they had been best friends since they were children and what kind of best friend would she be if she did not rejoice when they did. No, Sabina was determined to make the most out of their time together. Little did she know that they would find adventure along the way.

2

Drinks at Steveo's

After they went through customs, Marla asked the ticket agent about how they could get to their bungalow without walking there, he suggested a mass-transit van, and the girls thanked him. They had rented two bungalows - a two bedroom one for Marla and Lydia and a studio for Sabina.

Once they got settled, they headed to Steveo's Tiki Seafood and Bar. It was a quaint, outdoor restaurant that I worked at. I was only twenty-four at the time and still had not figured out what I wanted to do with my life. In fact, one may say I "wasted" my life away - in the day, I surfed, at night, I waited tables at the restaurant. I was the stereotypical "beach bum", but I didn't care. Before Sabina walked into my life, there was nothing that I had to look forward to, after I met her my life changed.

It was a slow night that evening; we only had six customers - peak season started two weeks later. Steveo was in the back barking orders at the cook, Ephino. I was in the front breathing on cups and I was "fog-writing", you know, writing on the cups while the fog from my breath lingered. I was uninterested in work that night - during peak season was when the international tourists came - other times of the year, it was only locals who ate at Steveo's.

I heard the women laughing as they walked in, but I remained disconnected, I sighed and walked up to their table. "Hi, welcome to Steveo's - we serve the best seafood on the island - may I get you anything to drink?" I sullenly repeated the same words I said every time that I waited on a customer.

"I'll have lemonade," Marla said to me.

"Make that two lemonades," Lydia repeated.

Sabina didn't say anything. At that point, I hadn't even realised that she was there - that's how disconnected I was. "Okay, two lemonades for the ladies. Coming right up."

"Wait…" Sabina finally spoke up. "I will try

your Twisted Strawberry, Rum and Lime Margarita."

That made me take notice. I remember thinking, *Hmm, the lady is adventurous.* I grinned at her and went back to get their drinks.

When I was in the back, I overheard the conversation that they were having. Lydia had a brochure for the island out on the table. I heard the words "Star of the Sea" and my interest was instantly piqued. A few months before that, a mysterious man had come to Steveo's. He was carrying a map in his right hand, and in his left, he carried a book. He had asked me if I knew where Steveo was and I directed him to the kitchen, Steveo closed the door and had spoken in low tones. The only words I could make out were "Star of the Sea", "treasure" and "adventure".

I had snuck into the kitchen from around the back and saw the man give Steveo what he had in his hands. Steveo had placed the book on the counter and pocketed the map. I had forgotten about all of that until I heard the girls talking that evening.

I walked back over to them and questioned them, "Are you girls talking about the treasure or the Star of the Sea?"

They blinked a few times and Sabina seemed startled. "Why, yes, we are. Do you know anything about it?"

"Well," I begun hesitantly, I wasn't sure how much to tell them. "My boss was given a book about it." I didn't mention the map as I felt that giving away the secret of his map may have ended up getting me fired. "He caught me looking at it a while back and told me to never try to find it again. From what I know, the Star of the Sea is some sort of treasure that was lost at sea in the 1600s. It hasn't been seen since." I finished sharing the story in a mysterious tone, it was my hope that the girls wouldn't get involved. It seemed like a dangerous secret and I didn't want them to get hurt while searching for it.

"Great," Marla spoke up. "Where is the

book now?"

I stopped for a moment and pondered, "Umm… well, the last I saw, he…"

At that moment, Steveo came out from the kitchen and I stopped speaking. He looked at me and called me back to his office, which was next to the kitchen. I looked at the girls and they smiled at me.

Sabina said, "Oh well, maybe you can tell us next time. We got to go. Thanks for the drinks and the enticing story, we'll talk to you later."

The others took the cue and stood up. They began walking away as Steveo called me again. I looked from him to them a few times before I decided to ask them how long they were staying.

Lydia's eyes sparkled teasingly, "We're staying a few days, Sabina's here for the entire summer. We'll be back tomorrow. Have a great night."

3

Curiosity and the Cat

I trudged back to Steveo's office. I was afraid that he had heard our discussion but it turned out that he only wanted to talk to me about how disconnected I had been at work. He threatened to fire me. I just rolled my eyes and my shift ended.

The next day, he called me and told me he was closing the restaurant down for a few days because his sister was sick, it was only later that I found out he never had a sister. It was my guess that during those few days he was actually searching for the treasure. At the time,

I had welcomed the impromptu vacation and decided to surf.

Those few days were wonderful, the waves were just right, but, I couldn't stop thinking about the treasure. Those girls had piqued my curiosity once again in the treasure and the desire to know about it swelled within me.

I went to the internet café down the street from Steveo's and typed "Star of the Sea" in a search engine, but nothing came up. I didn't know it at the time but it was a closely guarded secret and there was not a lot of information about it except for that book which had been written in the late 1880s and wasn't listed on the internet.

Curious, I thought to myself. *I wonder why that information is not public knowledge. Why isn't the book listed online?*

Being young and carefree, I decided to use my key and sneak into Steveo's. I reasoned that it wasn't breaking and entering since I had a key. However, on my way, I ran into - and I do mean literally ran into - Sabina. She was on the beach taking photographs of the sunset and I was in my own mind, muddling over the treasure. I ran smack dab into her back and her camera flew in the air.

She fell on the ground and I turned around, she began to yell at me, "WHAT DO YOU THI..." Then, she smiled. "Hey, it's you. From the other night, right? Treasure boy?" She pointed at me.

I bent down and grabbed her hand. I helped her to her feet, "Oh, I am so sorry. I am glad to see you again. Sabrina, right?"

She laughed as she brushed herself off. "No, SabINA; it's okay, a lot of people get those names confused. Sabina is not a common name." She smiled at me. "But, I never did get your name..."

I felt embarrassed and turned red. "Oh, my name is Max. Max Callaway. It's nice to meet you, Sabina whatever-your-last-name-is." I laughed a little bit. I always laughed when I felt embarrassed.

"Calli. Sabina Calli's the name."

"Where are your friends? I thought you guys came together?"

"Don't you remember..." She paused. "I mean, not like you should remember or anything, you probably have a lot of customers. They went home today, they were only here for the week. They told you that before you went into your boss' office the other night." It was her turn to turn ruddy. She seemed embarrassed, as well.

"Oh, that's right. Sorry about that. I have been thinking a lot about the treasure."

Her face lit up. "The treasure! Have you found anything else about it?"

I shook my head. "No, not yet. The oddest thing happened, I went online and searched about it but it is not listed there at all."

"Maybe somebody is hacking the system. I know, I know. I'm overly paranoid. It's my journalistic side. I studied journalism in college, just graduated. I want to work some day as the lead reporter for a world famous newspaper." Her eyes gleamed with excitement as she spoke about her desire. "Alas, who knows if that will ever happen." She added sadly.

I smiled. "Well, maybe if we figure this mystery out you can begin your career!" I offered, although, I was just trying to be nice.

"Well, Mr Callaway, you better remember to

find me if you discover anything else." She winked at me.

"I will." I nodded. "I am going to Steveo's now to do some detective work."

"Alrighty then, I will let you be." She began to turn away.

"Wait! How can I reach you if the mystery reveals more clues?"

She grinned. "I am staying at those bungalows over there." She pointed to a group of them about 50 yards away. "I am in number 5. Just come and knock on my door."

"Will do." We smiled at each other and I walked toward Steveo's.

4

The Adventure Begins...

It was that evening that the adventure truly began. As I went into Steveo's, I rummaged through the papers in his office, but soon, I heard murmurings in the hallway. I peaked out from behind the door only to hear Steveo's voice on the phone. He was using the one that was on the other side of the kitchen, so I grew quieter.

As he continued to talk, I went once more through his paperwork. I was looking for the book, it never appeared but on the top of his desk, there was an outline of this island and the waters around it. I quickly grabbed it, only to see that it was the treasure map. Then I stepped back from the desk and tripped over the chair! My heart pounded. I was afraid he had heard.

For what seemed like an eternity, I remained there as a sitting duck - he stayed on the phone and didn't hear. I was in luck. Then, as I turned away from the chair, I bumped into the side of the desk - that he heard! I listened to him tell the person on the other end to hold on and I held my breath. I looked for a place to hide but there was nowhere I could in his small office. I was doomed.

The door opened and Steveo flicked on the light. "What do you think you're doing in my office?"

"I... umm... I..." Unfortunately, I couldn't come up with a good excuse, so I told the truth. "Why are you acting so secretive about this map? Isn't it illegal to harbour information like this? Who was that man?"

He rolled his eyes as he approached me. He was only an inch from my face. "You have no right questioning me. I will do what I want, when I want. Don't question me about who that man was, that is for me to know."

He went to grab the map and I did all that I knew to do at the time, I ran. Perhaps it was a dumb thing to do, but remember, I was still young and naive. I had no idea that my boss was entangled in such evil activity.

I ran and ran until I reached the only person who would believe me about the map - Sabina. It was nine at night and I probably looked like a fool running to her place, but boy, I will never regret that decision.

I pounded furiously on her door and yelled, "Sabina, Sabina. It's Max. Open up."

Sabina's light flickered on and there was some movement inside. Before she answered, I heard Steveo coming up behind me. I looked back, he had wild eyes filled with fury. I screamed. "Hurry, hurry! Open up, Sabina."

She opened the door and I rushed in, practically pushing her over. I slammed the door only ten seconds before Steveo pounded at it. Sabina's right eyebrow was raised and she appeared befuddled.

"What's wrong, Max?"

"I... I got entangled with something... look, look, I found the map!" I tried to say catching my breath.

She smiled and took the map out of my hand. Then led me into the dining room - we were so enthralled in discussion that we hadn't even realised that Steveo had stopped pounding.

"So, we have the map..." Sabina looked up

at me ten minutes later. "Will we go exploring?" Her eyes twinkled.

"Don't you think we should give this map to the authorities? Obviously Steveo is doing something illegal and we should hand it in so that we aren't put into the same category as him." I tried really hard to reason with her.

"I suppose you're right." She sighed. "We'll call them now and tell them about the map, it is probably a national treasure!"

We phoned them and they said they would be over in a few minutes. Sabina made coffee for me as we waited.

Twenty minutes later, the door bell rang. I

opened it and saw the same man whom had given Steveo the map standing before me. I gasped as he raised his gun at me. Everything happened so fast that I do not remember much of it; I only know what Sabina told me happened. He raised his gun, shot me in the shoulder (although it was merely a graze), and tried to tackle me to the ground.

"You will never survive this. The Star of the Sea is worth a fortune and we will steal it at all cost." He had me pinned to the ground.

I struggled but I finally managed to get away. Sabina was crying and as I moved in to grab the map, the man tackled me again. I yelled, "Sabina, get it! Run!"

"Not over my dead body." He jumped over me and went after Sabina. She kicked him and he fell to the ground. She grabbed my hand and we ran out of the bungalow.

He didn't give up pursuit. We ran through the streets of Port Vila. There was a wedding reception in which we pretty much totalled, they were cutting the cake outside, and we had to dodge through it. Some of the cake splattered onto us, but we continued to run (of course, we yelled our apologies). He now was in hot pursuit of us. Sabina was getting winded, I had a strong pain that surged through my shoulder. I winced and she pointed us in the direction of an off-the-beaten-track road. We veered and managed to escape our pursuer.

Sabina climbed over a fence, helping me up with my good arm. Once we were on the other side, we stopped to catch our breath.

"Are you okay?" she asked me solemnly.

"I am just in a little pain, I will be okay. I've been in worse situations. The waves hurt more than this." I laughed vaguely.

She frowned. "Max, you are not okay. We need to stop and figure out what to do."

"Sabina, the most important thing here is that we protect this treasure, find it, and return it to the people of Vanuatu. I don't know what else to do, but it is not safe to return to your place, at the moment. We will go to mine;

Steveo never knew where I lived."

"Isn't your address listed on your employee forms?" she asked quizzically.

I chuckled. "I gave my mum's address." My eyes danced with child-like playfulness.

She giggled. "Why did you do that?"

"Because, if I want to surf and don't show up for work, I don't want him to be able to find me." I winked at her. "Come on, I will take you to my place."

5

Wrong Move

I led her to my apartment and we stayed up most of the night talking about the treasure.

Finally, Sabina got tired and I told her she could go up to my room and sleep, I slept on the couch. Around seven in the morning, my cell phone rang.

"Hello?"

A deep voice answered, "Hello, Max, this is Steveo. Look, I'm willing to deal with you. If you and your lady friend give me the treasure map, we can split the proceeds 50-50."

"Okay," I mumbled to him before I realised

what I had said. I was exhausted and half asleep. "Sure, we'll meet you at my place." I proceeded to give him my address.

"Wonderful." He hung up.

I laid on the couch for a few moments and then, I jumped up. *What did I say?* I thought to myself.

"Sabina!" I yelled. "Sabina, wake up!"

I heard her yawn. "What, Max? It's only…" She had looked at the clock. "It's only 7.15. I'm tired," she grumbled.

"I… made a mistake. Steveo called and I told him where I live. He's coming over!"

"WHAT?" she screamed. "What did you do that for?"

"I was half asleep. Come on, I am certain that you have said something when you were half asleep that you regretted."

She paused for a second, then, a shade of red appeared on her face. "Oh yeah, oh yeah. Okay, so, what do we do?"

As she asked that question, the door bell rang.

"It's him!"

"Is there any other way out of here?"

I thought for a second. "No, only the front door. We have to answer it."

"Okay, but hold on." Sabina pocketed the treasure map in her jacket. "Now, answer it."

I went to the door and opened it but Steveo

pushed it wide open. "Where is the map?"

I shuffled my feet. "We... lost it."

Sabina stepped forward, "Yes, we lost it. Sorry, man. Our mistake."

"YOU DIDN'T? THAT TREASURE IS WORTH MILLIONS. I'M GOING TO KILL YOU, MAX CALLAWAY!" He lunged at me. Then, he looked at Sabina. "Or maybe, I will take your friend." He grabbed her shoulders. "I could think of some things to do to her." He laughed.

I rammed into him and grabbed Sabina's hand. We ran out the front door. Steveo followed us once he regained his strength. We ran through a crowded market and knocked down some fruit on the vendor's tables. Again, we apologised but had to run faster as he was gaining up on us. We veered in and out of streets but couldn't lose him, until we saw a ferry that was about to leave.

"Let's grab it; do you have any money on you? I left mine at home," I asked her.

"I have my debit card and a few hundred dollars cash." She fingered through her pockets looking for cash.

Steveo was closing in but when he saw us get on the ferry, he gave up the chase and back-pedalled. The ferry captain looked at us and smiled. "In a bit of a bind, hmm?"

"Don't ask. Just please get us away from

the shore."

The other customers on the boat were staring at us; after all, we were a mess. Sabina's long brown hair had fallen out of her bun and was haphazardly upon her head, covered in sweat. My clothes were wrinkled and the blood spot from the previous night had dried, leaving me looking like a hobo. Eventually, they stopped staring and we were able to look at the treasure map.

"What do we know so far?" I asked.

"Well, there is a treasure and the police - and Steveo, of course - are trying to keep it secret. We have to find the treasure so that the nation can get the wealth from it. It is our duty now."

I reluctantly agreed with her. We continued looking at the map for five minutes and then, I had an idea. "Wait, Sabina, this place here." I pointed at a particular part of the map. "This place is only a mile from here." I moved my finger to an alcove about a mile away. "Maybe we could get off and go diving for it?"

Sabina looked amused. "Yes! Look, the water there must only be ten - fifteen feet down. We could dive for it easily - even without scuba gear! But, we have a problem." She pointed to the ferry captain. "I don't know if he will let us off or not."

"Let's ask him!" I walked up to the front of the boat and interrupted the captain. "Excuse me, sir? Is there a way my friend and I could be dropped off at that alcove there?" I pointed to it. "Could you pick us up later?" I paused. "We will pay you more!"

The captain hesitated for a second. "Of course. However, I can't pick you both up until tomorrow. Is that okay?"

I bit my lip and called Sabina over. Once she was by my side, I asked her, "Is it okay if we stay the night on the island? He's unable to return until tomorrow."

She smiled. "Of course." She turned to the captain. "You better pick us up tomorrow, though. Don't forget about us," she teased.

6

Adventure under the Sea

A strange look came into his eyes, but only for a second. "Of course, trust me, I wouldn't leave you." He gave a haphazard grin.

"Okayyyy." My eyebrow was raised and Sabina shrugged her shoulders. We got dropped off.

"Umm, what was that all about?" I continued saying as the boat left.

"Heck if I know… oh well, we have work to do."

We pinpointed the exact location that the treasure map showed and I decided to take the first dive. She agreed and waited by the shore as I went below the water. As I reached the bottom of the sea, I couldn't see anything at first. I almost gave up when something glistened at me.

I came up for air and went back down. This time I dug at the sand. There it was - a massive diamond! I was shocked. I grabbed it but it fell again because of the weight, I had to go get air anyhow.

I came up and called Sabina over. She bounced over to me and we dove in together. She went beneath the diamond and I went above it, we hauled it out of the sandy dune and came up for air. She was ecstatic.

"Oh my gosh!" she screamed. "It's real! The diamond is real! It's huge." We carried it to land.

"Whoa, check it out!" I exclaimed as I pointed at it. "No wonder they call it the Star of the Sea, it reflects the sun so beautifully!" The rays from the diamond seemingly jumped into the air. It left patterns of sun-reflected beauty all over me, Sabina, and the beach. It was a prism of light.

Sabina jumped through the light beams and joked, "Look at me, I'm walking on light!"

It was then that I noticed her beauty, perhaps it was the way the reflection caught in her hair or the joy that she exuded, but she struck my heart as more than just a fellow treasure seeker, she was - and is - a beautiful woman.

Her navy blue eyes were mixed with a hint of playfulness, adoration, joy, but also had shades of depth, understanding and wisdom. Her chestnut brown hair caught my eye, it was shoulder length and her body was curvy in all the right places. They say that one can fall in love with just one glance but I never believed that - until I met her. I can honestly say I fell in love with Sabina that day. I longed to spend the rest of my life with her. Everything about her captured my heart and brought joy to my soul.

I remember jumping up and dancing with her in the light for what seemed like an eternity. We were two carefree individuals, enjoying life and finding joy in the simplest of things. My heart beat so fast that day, I remember wondering if I would have a heart attack. Yes, every glance from her eyes sparked a sense of wonderment within me. I was longing to be with her.

Suddenly, fear overtook me. We were returning the next day, I was afraid that since the mystery seemed to be solved that we would not be together any longer. I couldn't imagine - and I still can't imagine - not having her in my life. Sabina had become what I lived for, I didn't have any other reason to go on but she brought joy into my life. I didn't want our time together to end.

Finally, she collapsed and I suggested we find some fruits - I was very hungry. I went into the forest to look around and found some and when I returned, Sabina mentioned, "You know, Max. I'm really glad we found the diamond."

I was heartsick, all I could think was that she was glad to get rid of me. My thoughts turned sour but she interrupted them with the most beautiful thing to escape her lips, "I don't want this to be over because of you... I... umm... well..."

"I know, shh, I know." I placed a finger to her lips. "You don't have to say it. I know." I reached over to her, stared into her eyes, and kissed her gently on her lips. And to my amazement, she kissed me back. The innocence of our kiss was beautiful, it was short and sweet, yet, left me awe-struck and dare I say, lovesick? She giggled and I held her hand. The sun was setting and we talked throughout the night.

We learned about our life and our desires, we learned about what made us both tick. We laughed, we cried, we shared stories of joy and sorrow, it was our first day of the rest of our lives. By three am, we had nothing left to say, instead, we held one another and Sabina fell asleep in my arms. Life was finally perfect.

7

The Rescue

The next day, Sabina wrapped the diamond in her jacket and we prepared to board the boat. She leaned over to me and asked, "Do you think we can continue last night for the rest of the summer?" She smiled as she searched my eyes.

I put my arm around her. "I think we can and I believe we will continue for a long time." I kissed her nose.

A few moments later, the ferry came into our view. We smiled at one another as it approached the shore.

The captain tipped his hat toward us and

yelled over the waves, "Nice day, isn't it? Here, let me help you."

He leapt out of the boat and came toward us - however, he was not alone. Two other men appeared from beneath the boat and he pointed to us. Before we knew what had occurred, the men had jumped us and held us against our will.

The captain laughed. "You really thought you could escape Steveo, didn't you? You two stole his treasure and we are stealing it back." He grabbed the diamond from Sabina and tossed it to the man who held me captive. "Take them on the boat, boys." They obeyed and we entered the boat.

I spat at him, "You will never get away with

this!"

The captain leered at me. "We will. You see, I am Smithy - Steveo's brother. You crossed the wrong family."

"What!" I snapped at him but he just laughed as he slapped me.

Sabina looked at me helplessly and mouthed to me, "Just let them, don't fight."

I was afraid and for the first time, my carefree personality felt bridled. The boat led us to the harbour where Steveo was awaiting us.

"Welcome guys. I see you found my diamond." His brother handed it to him. "Well, isn't this just pleasant? Thanks guys. We are going to take this diamond now and escape.

Bro?" He looked at his brother and the ferry. He prepared to board but just at that moment, a siren was heard. Steveo and his gang looked bewildered. "Who tipped them off?" he shouted.

The cops came up to him. "Steveo?"

"Yes?"

"You are under arrest for hacking the internet illegally, removing information, stealing from the people of this great land, holding people against their will, and having a person shot. Come with me." The cop looked at us. "Thank you guys for finding our lost treasure. We appreciate it."

"But, how did you find out?" Sabina looked

at him in amazement.

"When one of our own went rogue, working for these guys," he spat at Steveo and his group, "we realised that something was going on and he eventually fessed up. He was removed from the police and given only six months jail. Due to his confession, these men won't be so lucky." He gazed at those in question solemnly.

"Okay, time to go." The cops rounded the others into the car. "Thanks again, guys."

After they drove away, I looked at Sabina. "Now what?"

She grinned. "We surf!"

I laughed. "We are on the same page!"

8

Party Time

Two weeks later, the police contacted us and invited us to a party. It was about the returned diamond. We were thrilled to go, but when we got there, we each had a surprise waiting for us. The police had gone through Sabina's records and found out about her passion for journalism and had invited the producer of her favourite news network to come to the party.

He approached Sabina as soon as she arrived. Her eyes grew wide. "Miss Calli, I presume? My name is..."

She screamed, "David Balmer! I know who

you are. Oh my gosh! Your news network is my favourite. You are like my idol."

He smiled. "You, young lady, are my idol - I heard all about your investigation into the crime here and I want to offer you a job - how would you like to be an anchorwoman for our channel?"

"Are... are... you serious? Am I on *Candid Camera*? Am I being pranked? Whoa, yes man!"

She jumped up and hugged him. Then, she turned to me. "Did you... know?"

I grinned. "They found out about the journalism and asked me what you wanted to do, I told them."

"You are the best." She jumped into my arms and hugged me.

"But, Mr Max Callaway, I have a surprise for you, too." David looked at me.

My brow furrowed. "What?" I asked suspiciously.

"Well, I have a friend who is a detective - I told him about what you and Sabina accomplished and he wants to hire you as a private eye; would you be up for that? You and Sabina would live in the same town." He winked at me.

"Wow, I... I... yes! That would be great. I'm not sure if I will be any good at it but I would love to try."

"And, on top of that," the police chief interrupted us. "The people of Vanautu would like to present you and Ms Sabina with this cheque - consider it payment for a job well done." He handed us a cheque written out for 100,000 dollars. "Spend it however you wish." He winked at me - they all knew what I wanted to spend it on. Sabina began crying and thanked them about a dozen times, I simply walked away and went to the singer. I asked him to play her favourite song and it came on.

She smiled at me and I asked her to dance. As we did, I looked into her eyes and kissed her. By the end of the song, I dropped to my knees, she stared at me.

"Ms Sabina Calli, I know we have only known each other for a short time but I am thoroughly in love with you. Will you become Mrs Sabina Callaway? You are the only treasure I need."

She gasped and began to weep, "I would not want to be anybody's else wife, you are the love of my life. You have sparked my days with joy."

We left a week later to go back to her home, began work three weeks later, and by the end of that year, six months to the day that we met each other, we wed. She has been my everything ever since then. I would be nothing without her.

Max Callaway began to cry and gave the

microphone back to his daughter as Sabina smiled at him.

Sabina came up to him and kissed him tenderly on his lips. She looked him in the eye, "Max Callaway, I would be nothing without you either. You are my greatest treasure."

www.ingramcontent.com/pod-product-compliance
Lightning Source LLC
Chambersburg PA
CBHW071211130626
46555CB00004B/1664

Coming January 2014

For more information:

Official site:

www.scuppari.com

Like us at:

www.facebook.com/scuppariromanceminis

Follow us on Twitter:

@s_cuppari

www.ingramcontent.com/pod-product-compliance
Lightning Source LLC
Chambersburg PA
CBHW071211130626
46555CB00004B/1664